ANNA'S
ATHABASKAN SUMMER

by Arnold Griese

illustrated by Charles Ragins

Boyds Mills Press

Both author and illustrator are indebted
to the Athabaskan people of interior Alaska—
our thanks for making this book possible.

Text copyright © 1995 by Arnold Griese
Illustrations copyright © 1995 by Charles Ragins

Published by Caroline House
Boyds Mills Press, Inc.
A Highlights Company
815 Church Street
Honesdale, Pennsylvania 18431
Printed in Mexico

Publisher Cataloging-in-Publication Data
Griese, Arnold.
    Anna's Athabaskan summer / by Arnold Griese ; illustrated by
Charles Ragins—1st ed.
[32]p. : col. ill. ;   cm.
Summary : A young Athabaskan girl and her family make the annual return to their fish camp
where they prepare for the long winter ahead.
ISBN 1-56397-232-8
1. Athapascan Indians—Juvenile fiction. 2. Indians of North America—Canada—Juvenile fiction.
[1. Athapascan Indians—Fiction. 2. Indians of North America—Canada—Fiction.] I. Ragins,
Charles, ill. II. Title.
    [E]   1995   CIP
Library of Congress Catalog Card Number 94-70679

First edition, 1995
Book designed by Tim Gillner
The text of this book is set in 13.5-point Clarendon Light.
The illustrations are done in watercolors.
Distributed by St. Martin's Press

10 9 8 7 6 5 4 3 2

This story was originally published in *Highlights for Children*.

To my only grandson, Dusty, and to my three
great-grandchildren, Timothy James, Cole, and Ashley Eve.
—A. G.

For Mom and Dad, with special thanks to the
Cline family of Nulato.
—C. R.

My world of winter is a world of snow, and of cold, and of darkness. It is a beautiful time, but for me it is a time of waiting. Waiting for the sun to warm the earth and to bring life again to our frozen land.

Then come warm days, pussy willows, melting snow, and the sound of birds. All this, and the breakup of ice on the river, tell me spring has come once again. The days go by quickly now, like the shadow of a soaring hawk. Soon school will be out.

One day Father takes Mother, Grandmother, Pup, and me in his boat to our summer fish camp. Mother says our people, the Athabaskan Indians, have always come to this place in summer. Here fish swim close to the shore, big berries grow on the hillside, and soft winds off the water blow the mosquitoes away.

When the boat touches the beach, I jump out and climb the hill, then sit, resting. A fox runs past, carrying food to its family. Far away, the mountain we call "Denali" stands tall in the clear air. In front of me the river flows forever.

Mother's call stops my dreaming, and I hurry back to the beach. The open door, curling smoke from the stove pipe, and the rattle of pans are all signs. Work is waiting. But today I want to play. Then I remember Mother is going to have a baby. I smile and go inside.

In the busy days that follow, many things are done. Mother and I clean the house. We put food from town in the cache where animals cannot get it. Grandmother lays out a moose hide to be worked on.

After going back to town to get the dogs, Father moves the fish wheel out into the fast current. Water gurgles as it pushes against the paddles that turn the wheel. The wheel groans and creaks as it moves.

Soon, the first swimming salmon will be scooped up in one of the baskets and dropped into the fish box. Then the hard work I do not like starts. The fish must be cleaned.

Now empty drying racks stand waiting. Father's dogs
are tied close by to keep bears away. Everything is ready.
It is time for Father to leave. His hand rumples my hair
as we walk to the boat. He and my older brother both
have jobs in town.

Grandmother is scraping the moose hide as I walk toward the house. I see that now it is hard for her to do the work she loves.

Mother calls from the smokehouse and I go to her. "There is not much work to do today," she says. "Take Grandmother to the place she loves and sit with her."

Grandmother and I go. While we sit looking down on our summer home, two ravens call to each other as they tumble through the air.

Grandmother looks up and says, "Old Grandfather, bring us luck."

"Why do you say that, Grandmother?"

She answers, "Our people say that Raven made the world. That, even though he plays tricks, he can bring luck."

The sun warms me as I watch the ravens. "What luck will they bring?" I ask myself.

Late that same night, while the midnight sun is low in the sky, I watch as the fish wheel scoops up the first summer salmon. It flops down into the waiting box. There the salmon's strong tail pounds against the sides.

Long ago, our people would hold a feast for the first salmon. It meant more were coming. These salmon would supply food for the long winter to come.

Soon after, our fish box fills. Grandmother rests while she watches us clean fish during these long days of summer.

While I work, there is time to think. I hope the baby growing inside Mother is a girl. I could show a little sister the things I am learning from Mother.

One day I ask Mother, "Grandmother says we must show respect for all living things. Then why do we catch and kill the salmon?"

Mother brushes hair from her face and answers, "Our people believe living things die gladly for us. But we must show respect by killing only what we need and by returning to the river fish bones and other things we cannot eat."

After many days of hard work, the fish wheel brings us fewer salmon. Now Grandmother and I can walk to the hillside where big blueberries wait to be picked. The sun warms our backs as we kneel and pull the berries into our buckets. Grandmother watches as some of the berries find their way into my mouth. The quiet is broken as we laugh. It is good to hear Grandmother laugh the way she used to.

Once while we are picking blueberries, Grandmother puts
her hand on my shoulder. I look up, and her eyes tell me not to
move. She whispers, "A bear eats berries and does not see us."
Grandmother's hand stays on my shoulder as we crawl back
slowly. Today the berries belong to the bear.

Early one morning, rain falling on the tin roof wakes me. Low gray clouds fill the sky. The air is chilly. I snuggle back under the covers.

After a while I go to walk in the rain. Ripe, red cranberries hang on the bushes along the bank. Their sweet smell fills the air.

Now, as Grandmother and I pick cranberries, the sky is deep blue, the air smells different, and the days grow shorter. The nights are dark again. Summer is ending.

Not many mornings later it comes—the cry of geese. I leave my warm bed and stand outside the door. In the sky, long lines of geese call to each other as they fly to warmer places.

The pebbles are cold under my bare feet as I walk to the beach. A spruce hen flies up. The leaves on the birch tree where it lands have turned golden.

That night, while Mother packs, I walk with Grandmother along the water in the soft light of a full moon. The warm glow from Mother's lamp shines through the window. It brings a special stillness. The soft sound of an owl's call floats through the air.

We go inside and I ask Grandmother, "Why does summer have to end?"

She answers, "Summer will come again as it always has since our people have lived by this river and fished on its banks." She stops, then adds, "Nothing ends. Someday I will leave you. But that is not the end. I will always be a part of your life."

I walk over and give her a hard hug. She holds me close for a long time.

The next morning, the sound of a motor from across the river reaches my ears. This time Father will take us home. Summer is over. It does not take long to load our things.

Bundled in my warm jacket, I take one last look at our summer home. But the sadness leaves me as I hold Grandmother tight.

When summer comes again we will come back and bring someone new. Someone I can teach about the ways of our people.

The Creepy Caves Mystery

This book belongs to:

Warrior _____

will, God's Mighty Warrior™
series includes:

Will, God's Mighty Warrior™
The Mystery of Magillicuddy's Gold
The Creepy Caves Mystery

And just for girls:
gigi, God's Little Princess™
series includes:

Gigi, God's Little Princess™
(in book and DVD formats)
The Royal Tea Party*
The Perfect Christmas Gift
The Pink Ballerina*
The Purple Ponies
Gigi's Hugest Announcement DVD
(*indicates stories that appear on this DVD)

will

God's Mighty Warrior™

The Creepy Caves Mystery

By Sheila Walsh
Illustrated by Meredith Johnson

THOMAS NELSON
Since 1798

NASHVILLE   DALLAS   MEXICO CITY   RIO DE JANEIRO   BEIJING

WILL, GOD'S MIGHTY WARRIOR™: THE CREEPY CAVES MYSTERY
Text © 2008 by Sheila Walsh.
Illustrations © 2008 by Thomas Nelson, Inc.

Published in Nashville, Tennessee, by Thomas Nelson. Thomas Nelson is a trademark of Thomas Nelson, Inc.

Thomas Nelson, Inc., books may be purchased in bulk for educational, business, fund-raising, or sales promotional use. For information, please e-mail SpecialMarkets@ThomasNelson.com.

Will, God's Mighty Warrior™ is a trademark of Sheila Walsh, Inc. Used by permission.

Scripture quoted from the *International Children's Bible*®, *New Century Version*®, © 1986, 1988, 1999 by Thomas Nelson, Inc., Nashville, Tennessee 37214.

Library of Congress Cataloging-in-Publication Data
Walsh, Sheila, 1956–
  The Creepy Caves Mystery / Sheila Walsh ; illustrated by Meredith Johnson.
     p. cm. — (Will, God's mighty warrior)
  Summary: When young Will, seeking adventure while visiting his grandparents, hears strange noises coming from a cave and leads "Detective Ralph," his dog, to investigate, even though Papa said to wait for him, he comes to understand more about God and being obedient.
  ISBN-13: 978-1-4003-1125-5 (hardcover)
  ISBN-10: 1-4003-1125-X
  [1. Obedience—Fiction. 2. Caves—Fiction. 3. Grandparents—Fiction. 4. Dogs—Fiction. 5. Christian life—Fiction.] I. Johnson, Meredith, ill. II. Title.
  PZ7.W16894Cre2007
  [E]—dc22
                              2007029354

Printed in China
08 09 10 11 12 MT 5 4 3 2 1

This book is
dedicated to Christian
Walsh and to Chase, Cole,
and Tate Trammel—if there
is a mystery to be
uncovered, these boys
will find it!

"Ralph and I were born for adventure," Will announced to his grandparents, Nana and Papa, on the first day of his summer visit."

"We are SO ready.
First, we'll chase sand crabs and
look for jellyfish . . .

then we'll swim . . .

then we'll look for clues to any unsolved
mysteries . . . and then we'll have lunch."

"I brought everything I need to solve a mystery."

✓ A notebook to record anything out of the ordinary

✓ Binoculars to spy on suspicious characters

✓ A pen that is actually a camera

✓ A listening device disguised as headphones

"Ralph, you will need to learn to creep very quietly,"
Will said, and he proceeded to show Ralph what creeping
quietly looked like.

"Well, let's start at the beach where you can play in the ocean or build sandcastles," Nana said.

"Sandcastles!" Will said, horrified at the very idea. "That might be Princess Gigi's idea of fun, but Ralph and I are here to meet adventure and danger face-to-face."

"Ah," Papa said, "I know just where to take you . . .

Creepy Caves."

"Did you say . . . Creepy Caves?" Will asked, hardly able to contain his excitement.

"Yes," Papa replied. "Legend says that Creepy Caves used to be a hideout for robbers and that sometimes at night you can still hear noises and see light coming from the largest cave."

"Detective Ralph and I are on the case!" Will said.

"Listen, Will, Creepy Caves can be dangerous. You need to wait for me to go with you. You and Nana go to the beach this morning, and I will come at lunch to take you and Ralph to Creepy Caves. Now, don't go into the caves without me."

All morning Will and Ralph splashed in the water and chased sand crabs on the beach near Creepy Caves.

"The caves don't look very creepy," Will whispered to Ralph. "At least not to a fearless detective like me."

Ralph agreed with a happy woof.

"I can't believe we can see Creepy Caves and have to wait for Papa to go inside them," Will muttered.

Suddenly Will heard a strange noise coming from inside the caves. It sounded like something scratching across rock. "That must be the robbers hiding their treasure! There is something mysterious going on in that cave." Will looked through his binoculars and gasped when he saw footprints at the cave entrance. "Ralph, we are fearless detectives! We must investigate."

"I have my camera. I could take a photograph of the robber, and we'll turn him in," Will said in a tough voice. "Papa said to wait for him. But if we wait, the robber might get away." Ralph growled at the thought.

Will crept up to the cave. Ralph crept close behind just like Will had taught him.

"It's dark in there," Will whispered. "I wish I had my flashlight."

"We'll just take a quick look inside. It wouldn't really be bad if we just went in a little way," Will reasoned.

Will was wrong about that!

Inside the cave, the path quickly turned to the left. It was very dark.

Ralph whined.

"Do not fear, Detective Ralph," Will said in a
shaky voice. "I'm right here, boy . . . just stay close beside me."

Will heard footsteps and began to think that this had been
a very bad idea. The robbers must be coming after him!
He turned to run.

Suddenly he tripped and fell onto the jagged rocks.
Will scraped his hands and knees. He couldn't see a thing.
Something fluttered in the air right by his face.

Detective Will screamed. He thought to himself, *Papa told me not to come in the cave without him, and now I'm lost, it's dark, robbers are chasing me, and there's a ginormous bird that's going to eat me!*

Will heard footsteps coming right toward him. A light shone in his face. Then he saw Papa kneeling down to him.

"Papa!" Will cried.

"I am right here, Will," Papa said.

From farther inside the cave, a voice called out, "Hey, who's there?"

"Run, Papa, run! It's a stinking, rotten robber and his killer pterodactyl," Will cried out.

Just then a young man appeared.

"Don't be scared! I'm Mike Stone," he said. "I'm a college student studying the life of bats! Lots of them live in this cave."

"Wow! Bats! That must be what swooped by my head! But what was that weird noise?" Will asked.

"I scraped against the cave rocks with my ladder," Mike answered.

"Now it all makes sense!" Will exclaimed. "The Creepy Caves Mystery is solved!"

Mike told them lots of fun things about bats like the fact that they have fur all over their bodies. He asked Will and Papa to come back the next afternoon to watch him work.

After Mike left, Will and Papa headed for the picnic lunch Nana had waiting for them on the beach.

"Papa, I'm sorry that I went into the caves when you told me
not to," Will said.

"I forgive you, Will. Let's give it another try. But this time we'll
go together and meet Mike to see those bats. Now *there's* another
mystery: How did God make something as amazing as bats?"

"God is SO cool!" Will said with a grin. "And I am SO on the case."

That night after his Creepy Caves adventure, Will prayed . . .

*Dear God, thank You for today. Thank You that
Papa was there when I needed him. I'm glad You're
always with me too. I'm sorry that I disobeyed.
Please help me see some bats tomorrow. And it
would be great if they were friendly and
didn't poop on my head.
Amen.*

Children, obey
your parents the way
the Lord wants. This is
the right thing to do.
Ephesians 6:1